RUPERT

and the
NUTWOOD WELL

CARNIVAL

"You must have dressed in a hurry this morning, Rupert - the buckle on your shoe is undone," says Rupert's friend, Bill Badger.

Rupert glances down at his feet and Bill jumps with glee. "April Fool!" he cries.

"Crumbs," gasps Rupert. "Is it April the first today? I had completely forgotten."

Bill chuckles. "Let's look for Algy and Edward," he says. "I'm sure they will have forgotten too. We can play the same trick on them."

The two pals set off for Nutwood
Common. But along the way they
meet a very worried-looking Willie
Mouse.

"Have you heard the terrible
news?" he quavers.
"Why, whatever is the matter?"
exclaims Rupert.

"The matter? Nobody is allowed on the Common any more, that's what's the matter," cries Willie.

He points to a big board with official-looking writing on it.

Bill looks puzzled. "What does it mean?" he asks.

"It seems they're going to dig for oil here," says Rupert thoughtfully.

Bill looks aghast. "You mean - there's going to be an OIL WELL on the Common?"
"I told you we couldn't play here any more," moans Willie.

The friends stare at each other gloomily. Suddenly Tigerlily, the little Chinese girl, rushes up. "Why you look so sad?" she demands.

Rupert points to the sign and Tigerlily claps her hands in delight. "Is good news we have oil in ground," she cries. "It mean I can wear new dress every day!"

Her friends look puzzied.

"I see plenty pictures of people with
oil in ground," she says excitedly.
"Everybody wear overalls and
helmets except ladies.

Ladies have lots of pretty clothes and eat breakfast by swimming pool!"
"I don't think it's like that in real life," says Rupert doubtfully.

"And anyway," objects Bill, "you don't have a swimming pool." Tigerlily frowns. "Is small problem- yes," she admits. " I talk to my Daddy about it." She dashes off, leaving the chums gasping.

"I don't have to wear a helmet, do I?" asks Willie. "I'd look silly."
"YOU look silly anyway, so it won't make any difference," snaps a voice.

It is Pong-Ping, the peke, out for his
morning walk. He looks very cross.

"Why is everyone in my way this morning? I come here for peace and quiet, and find CROWDS everywhere." "Have you seen the sign?" asks Rupert.

Pong-Ping sniffs. "No, and I don't want to. I have better things to do, and so should you."

He stomps off, and Rupert feels gloomier than ever! "It won't be much fun if we can't go on the Common any more," he sighs.

But suddenly, Rupert looks at the sign again - and begins to wonder.

If the letters in PRO-FAL OIL are re-arranged, they make ...APRIL FOOL! "Oh no," he gasps. "Could it be a hoax?"

"Ha, ha, ha." Algy Pug and Edward
Trunk leap out from some nearby
bushes laughing loudly. "April Fool,
Rupert," they cry.

"My Dad and I built the board and painted it for April Fool's Day," grins Algy. "Then Edward here put it up for us. I'm sure we tricked EVERYONE!"

"Except ME," shouts Pong-Ping, back from his walk. "You can't catch ME that easily."

Algy looks at the peke innocently. "Crumbs, Pong-Ping," he exclaims. "I'm surprised you were able to walk so far with your shoe undone."

Pong-Ping glances down at his feet and - well, you can guess what the chums chorused, can't you?

Altogether now:
APRIL FOOL!

Carnival
An imprint of the Children's Division
of the Collins Publishing Group
8 Grafton Street, London W1X 3LA

First published by Dragon Books 1986
Published in this edition by Carnival 1989

Written by Len Collis
Illustrated by Jon Davis
Copyright © The Nutwood Press 1986
Copyright © title and character of Rupert Bear,
Express Newspapers plc 1986

ISBN 0 00 194455 X

Printed & bound in Great Britain by
BPCC Paulton Books Limited